D1473498

The
Storytelling
Star

The Storytelling Star

TALES OF THE SUN, MOON AND STARS

JAMES RIORDAN

Illustrated by
AMANDA HALL

PAVILION

First published in Great Britain in 1999 by
PAVILION BOOKS LIMITED
London House, Great Eastern Wharf
Parkgate Road, London SW11 4NQ

Illustrations © Amanda Hall 1999
Text © James Riordan 1999

Design and layout © Pavilion Books Ltd. 1999

Designed by Janet James

A CIP catalogue record for this book is available
from the British Library.

ISBN 186205 2026

Set in Garamond
Printed in Italy by Giunti Industrie Grafiche

2 4 6 8 10 9 7 5 3 1

This book can be ordered direct from the publisher. Please contact
the Marketing Department. But try your bookshop first.

CONTENTS

The Storytelling Star 11
Seneca

Birth of the Stars 15
Inca

The Loving Moon Star 18
Chippewa

The Girl Who Became the Sun 24
Aztec

The Making of Heaven and Earth 29
Maori

Battle of the Northern Lights 34
Saami

The Little Master Thief 41
Norse

Perseus and Andromeda 45
Ancient Greece

Seventh Day of the Seventh Moon 51
China

Sources 58

The Storytelling Star

✳◀ S E N E C A ▶✳

There was once a young man who used to travel the land working here and there; and he would stay the night along the way in friendly lodges. Yet he soon found that he was not so welcome in these places, for his fellow travellers expected him to keep the night going with a story.

But he had none at all to tell.

Now, one evening he was walking along looking for somewhere to stay the night. It was getting dark and since no one would give him a bed in a lodge, he decided he would have to sleep in the forest. Feeling tired, he made for a clearing in the trees and sat down with his back against an oak.

Above him the dark blue sky glittered with bright stars and a round white moon.

As he was sitting there, eating a supper of roots and berries, he suddenly heard a deep, deep voice say, 'Shall I tell you a story?'

He looked up, expecting to see a man standing before him. Seeing no one, he thought it must be the wind, and he went back to eating his meal.

'Shall I tell you a story?' came the voice again.

There could be no doubt: someone had spoken. He peered in all directions, yet saw nobody. Clearly, some rascal was playing tricks on him. So he got up and looked behind every tree and bush. There was no one there.

Puzzled, he went back to his oak tree. Yet he did not eat for fear of missing any more words. After a while, the voice came again: 'Shall I tell you a story?'

This time he knew: the voice came from a bright star in the sky. Glancing up, he saw the star gazing down on him.

'What do you mean? What kind of story?' he asked.

'Many stories that happened in the long-ago time,' the star replied.

'I'd love to hear a story,' the man said.

'Then let's strike a bargain: I'll tell you stories, and you will pass them on to others; and they will tell them from one generation to the next.'

'I'll do my best,' he said, eager to hear the tales. And he settled back to listen in the quiet of the night. The storytelling star began:

'Stories are like the stars in the sky: they are countless and last for time out of mind. Guard them well and treat them with care. For they can heal the sick, tame the wind and bring comfort to those who grieve.'

'Oh, I will, I will,' he said.

With some stories you'll remember every word I say, some only part, others you'll forget altogether. Listen closely.'

The young man bent his head and listened. Once in a while he said 'uhn' and nodded. The star told of how the stars came into the sky, how the Milky Way appeared, how a young girl became the sun, of the devoted moon star, the battle of the northern lights, and much besides. By the time the star had finished, the sun was almost up.

'There, my stories are all told,' it said. 'Tell them to your friends and to your children and your children's children, and so on down the years. And in future, when someone asks you for a story, tell them one from the Storytelling Star.'

And so it was. All the stories we know come from the Storytelling Star – and much of our wisdom too. As for the young man, he was now welcome everywhere he went, for he always had a tale to tell.

Birth of the Stars

There was once a time when not a single star shone in the long black night. At sunset each day, a wizard drew a curtain across the sky, casting the land into darkest gloom. Only at dawn did the curtain rise to reveal the bright warm sun.

Of an evening in those distant times, people would gather in a tent to watch as artists lit torches and held up wooden figures of birds and beasts. The light would throw giant shadows on the wall, making the figures dance and leap about.

One day the artists had an idea: why not cast shadows on to the curtain of the sky?

So that evening people gathered at the foot of a hill to watch the show. As darkness fell, the artists lifted their carved figures high so that the shadows, enlarged hundreds of times, played upon the black curtain of the night. Now everyone could see the sky shadows. And not only humans were watching.

Cats with kittens climbed up to the rooftops. Mice scurried into the topmost branches of the trees. Snakes stood on their tails to gain a better view. Even pigs and tortoises, who had never looked above their noses, lay on their backs to see the show.

Now, one time a little moth decided to take a peep behind the curtain. Climbing up the cloth, she set to nibbling a hole. Then, just as she made a gap for her head – BANG! – the wizard sent her spinning down again.

The little moth was stubborn. She flew straight back up and set to gnawing once again; and she made a hole before the wizard could drive her down.

Wonder of wonders! The sky watchers saw a light peeping through the hole. It was the first bright shining star.

The busy moth made more holes: a second and a third star appeared. Soon there were so many stars the people could not count them.

As the stars lit up the land, people could see mountain paths dotted with cactus plants and eucalyptus trees. They saw olive valleys, orange plains and silver streams. Then they noticed that the sky had changed colour: instead of black, it was now a navy blue – too light for the artists to perform their shadow show. But they did not mind.

After all, as the people gazed up at the starry sky, they were seeing the greatest picture show on earth.

The Loving Moon Star

CHIPPEWA

Long ago, in the dawning of the world, there was a village beside a lake. By day the people went about their work; and in the evenings they would gather upon the bank to watch the stars. For stars, they knew, were the homes of people who had passed into the spirit land. And the raindrops that fell were really tears falling from the tents up in the sky: the star people were sad.

One night, as the people looked into the sky, they saw a moon star brighter than all the others shining far away, at the very edge of the night sky. With every passing night, the moon star came closer, growing brighter all the time. Finally, it hung above the people by the lake, lighting up the fading embers of their fires as they prepared to sleep.

18

It made them afraid.

In the days to come, it would hang above the heads of little children, as if wishing to play. But their cries drove the moon star away. It tried to join in the young men's games; but they thought it was an evil spirit and fired their arrows at it.

How it longed to dance with the women, bobbing and gliding round the fire. But their angry shouts drove it off.

The moon star was very sad.

Among all the people of the lake only one was unafraid of the shining moon star. That was Powomis, a young girl who lived with her parents at one end of the lake. The moon star held no fear for her; she loved it with all her heart and never tired of playing in its bright rays.

The moon star clearly loved her too. For whenever Powomis went with her parents into the hills, or fishing in the lake, or picking berries and mushrooms in the woods, the moon star followed, lighting up the way. And when she awoke at night, there it was, hovering above her head. Many's the time she wished to reach up and touch it, but it stayed just out of reach.

Everyone wondered at the moon star's devotion; they were surprised to see its twinkling light guarding the young maid. Her father would always return from fishing with a good catch; her mother never came home from the forest without a basketful of nuts or berries.

'The moon star must be a good spirit,' they said.

From then on no one feared it any more. All the same, it never left its first fond friend.

Autumn came and transformed the forest on the hill above the lake: and it was beautiful beyond compare. The maple tree was afire with colour, gleaming in the autumn sun, with every shade of gold, brown and russet red. The slender leaves of the sumac tree were like scarlet tongues of fire. And with the fall of leaves, the nuts and berries ripened.

It was on an autumn morning that Powomis took her willow basket and went into the woods to gather fruit. At the forest edge the berries had been mostly eaten by birds and deer. So she pressed on into the forest depths. But amid the tangled vines and roots she lost her way and soon found herself wading into a swamp.

She shouted as loudly as she could; but no one heard her cries save the frogs and toads. As darkness fell, the water came up to her knees and the clinging mud tried to drag her down. She kept looking up, hoping to see the moon star she loved. But the sky was full of low black cloud that kept out the star's bright light. Soon drops of rain began to fall: they grew and grew until it seemed that all the stars were weeping without cease.

The waters of the swamp rose higher and higher, and soon swept poor Powomis off her feet. She was never seen again. Only her little basket was washed up on the shore close by her parents' tent.

As the days passed, the loving moon star shone even more brightly above the campfires round the lake. Yet it never stayed long in one place; it seemed restless, as if searching for something it could not find. Then, one night, it disappeared and was not

seen again until a young man had a dream. And in his dream he saw the moon star once more, but this time it had a young man's face, with tears glistening on his cheeks. In a sad, low voice, the handsome moon man spoke these words,

'Do tell me where Powomis is. If she still lives I will come down to earth and marry her; if she is dead, I shall guard her spirit all my days. Give me a sign.'

When the young man awoke from his dream, he hurried from his tent and gazed into the early morning sky. There was the moon star above him, blinking sadly as its silvery light faded with the dawn. An idea came to him: he would cast a crown of water lilies on the lake as sign of the young girl's fate.

Poor moon star. As he shone down that night he saw the dark ring of lilies on the silver lake and he knew his love's sad fate. All night long he grieved and then, before the dawn, his mind was made up.

'I shall watch over Powomis's people by the lake,' he sighed. 'I shall guard the babies as they sleep in their cradles; the little children will be my companions as they swim and play – I shall see they come to no harm. And I shall protect the spirit of Powomis in the sky.'

Next evening, as the people looked up at the dark blue sky, they saw the handsome moon man smiling down. And there, held in his pale arms, they clearly saw Powomis; her smiling eyes told them she was content.

The Girl Who Became the Sun

◆ AZTEC ◆

One time the earth was plunged into darkest gloom. No pearl-grey dawn, no lilac dusk, no golden days.

At last, the gods decided there must be light.

'We need a sun,' said one, 'to give life to Mother Earth and make the plants and flowers grow.'

'But too much sun will dry up lakes and streams,' another said.

'Then let a moon light up the land while the sun is at its rest. That way, the sun need shine for only half the day.'

It was agreed.

But who would be the sun and who the moon? Who would sacrifice their godly form?

At once, the God of Snails declared, 'I will be the sun; I will exchange my life for everlasting fame.'

He was big and strong and vain.

Yet no god or goddess wished to be the moon.

Anxiously the gods glanced around: there could be no sun without a moon. Finally, their gaze fell upon a young girl standing shyly in their midst. She was the Goddess of Sores. Her frail body, barely hidden by her ragged robe, was covered in red sores.

'If you agree,' they said, 'your light will guide the people's way – and your skin will be as smooth as silk.'

She smiled bravely. 'I would love to be the people's guide,' she softly said.

At once the gods began to build two tall stone pillars upon the mountain top: one for the sun, one for the moon. Meanwhile the God of Snails and the Goddess of Sores both bathed and oiled themselves; each then dressed in their own way.

The God of Snails covered his copper-coloured limbs with royal robes, put parrot plumes upon his head, a collar of gleaming gold about his neck, long jade earrings in his ears.

The Goddess of Sores had no fine robes. So she daubed her red-raw body white and put on a thin paper frock that barely hid her skinny form.

The gods had built a funeral pyre at the foot of the white pillars. So many logs blazed on the fire that the heavens glowed a ruby red, lighting up the two lone figures on the mountain top.

The God of Snails bit his lip in fear as he glanced down. Trembling, he drew back, while the girl stood still, clenching her tiny fists. He had chosen to leap first into the flames – that way he was sure to be the sun. At the gods' command he stepped towards the edge, standing tall and grand upon the pillar of white stone, his plumage blowing in the breeze.

Yet at the last moment his courage failed.

Three times they shouted 'Jump!' and three times he drew back from the brink.

Finally, the gods lost patience, turned to the girl and shouted, 'Jump!'

She stood unflinching at the edge, closed her eyes and leapt straight into the flames.

Afraid that the sun's power would not be his, the God of Snails shut tight his eyes and jumped into the fire after her. But in his haste, he fell to one side where the flames were weak and the ash was thick.

There, it was done. The gods were content.

But which one would be the sun?

The gods did not have long to wait for their answer.

From out of nowhere swooped an eagle, down into the red heart of the flames: in and out so quickly only its wingtips were singed. It soared upwards with a fiery ball in its beak, speeding like a burning arrow across the sky until it reached heaven's eastern gates.

There it set down the sun – for this is what the little goddess had become; and she took her seat upon a throne of snow-white clouds.

Her shining tresses were strung with gleaming gold shimmering in the mists of dawn. Her scarlet lips parted in a smile that sent warm, sparkling rays back down to earth.

Never was dawn so beautiful.

A great roar rose from the gods, rumbling like thunder through the morning sky.

Just then a white raven dived into the dying embers of the fire and was scorched as black as tar. It flew up with an ash-coloured ball of fire held firmly in its beak; and this it placed at heaven's western gates.

The earth now had a sun and moon.

Ever since that time, the eagle's wingtips have been dark brown and the raven is pitch black. And while the moon is always ashen white, the sun retains her bright red glow from the fire's heart.

The Making of Heaven and Earth

◆ MAORI ◆

In the long-ago time, before there was night and day, Rangi, Father Sky, held Papa, Mother Earth, tightly to him. Their many children could not see at all in the gloom; and they had to crawl on hands and knees because they had no room to stand.

Long years passed, and the children of Rangi and Papa were pale and bent. They longed for light, and for warm breezes to blow across the hills. At last, the children came together to decide what to do.

Tane, the strongest of them all, said, 'Let us push Father Sky away. Then it will be light and we can live close to Mother Earth.'

The others agreed.

First Rongo, god of harvests, pressed his shoulders against

Father Sky and tried to push him away. He strained hard, but could not move his father.

Tangaroa, god of the sea, tried next. But he could do no better. One after the other, the gods pushed and heaved, yet none could shift the sky. Finally, Tane rose up. He stood firmly on the earth and pressed his hands against the sky. Then he took a deep breath and pushed hard.

The air groaned between earth and sky, and Father Sky moved a little.

Tane strained again and, bit by bit, he moved the sky farther away. Light came flooding in, just as it does each morning when the sun peeps over the rim of the world. Up and up Rangi rose until his children could no longer see his face.

For the first time the gods could see all of Mother Earth.

A silver veil hung over her shoulders, and teardrops rained down on her as Rangi wept. But the gods rejoiced, for now they could move about and enjoy the beauty of the earth.

Although he had thrust his parents far away from each other, Tane loved them dearly; and he longed to make them happy.

Since he was god of the forest, he decided to plant trees all over the earth to keep his mother warm. The trees sank into the soil and took firm root, while their leaves rustled in the breeze and birds settled in the branches.

How lovely Mother Earth looked dressed in the leafy green of newly-planted trees. Father Sky looked down and smiled.

Towards evening, however, Tane noticed that his father was sad and grey; so Tane leapt up and set the red sun upon his back

and the silver moon upon his breast. When the sun shone down, Mother Earth smiled too as she gazed up at her bright husband. And when the sun disappeared and the sky grew dark, the moon shone down upon the hills and valleys. Both earth and sky were content.

'What else can I do to show my love?' Tane wondered. 'I know, I will bring the Shining Elves for Rangi.'

He travelled across hills and plains, over rivers and seas until he arrived at a place where there was neither land nor sea. On he went into the gloom until in the distance he saw a glimmer of light. Somewhere ahead of him was the tall mountain where his brother Uru lived with his children, the Shining Elves.

Uru welcomed Tane and asked news of their mother and father.

'I saw the sky rolled back,' Uru said. 'Even from here I saw the far-off glow of light between sky and earth. Now our Mother will be warm with the trees you have planted; some day men and women will come to live among the trees, and their children will swim in the great waves of the sea. They will grow food and take fish from Tangaroa. Surely your work is now done and you can rest.'

'Not yet, brother,' Tane said. 'Rangi lies dark and still at night. Will you let your children clothe him with living fire?'

Uru at once put his hands to his mouth and his voice rumbled down the mountain slopes like a thunder clap. The Shining Elves heard his call; they stopped their games and came hurrying up the mountain. Tane watched them as they approached. Each

Shining Elf glowed and twinkled, and the entire mountain was lit up as they came near.

Uru handed his brother a basket so that he could fill it full of Shining Elves. With the basket on his back, Tane sped through the gloom towards his father. And when he reached the sky, he took the basket and tied the Shining Elves to his father's cloak. He hung a bright light at each corner, and on the breast he placed five glowing lights in the form of a cross. The others he spread far and wide across the sky.

As for the basket, it still hangs there with Uru's remaining children. It is called the Milky Way. It is this soft light which protects little children through the night.

Battle of the Northern Lights

🌸 S A A M I 🌸

All through the day Sun rides through the sky in a golden sledge drawn by two reindeer and a polar bear. Towards dusk, when Sun grows weary, he sinks down to the sea to rest and regain his powers for the coming day.

One evening, as Sun descended to his watery couch, his son Peivalke came to him, saying, 'Father, it is time for me to wed.'

'Have you chosen a bride?' asked Sun wearily.

'Not yet. I have tried my golden boots on many earthly maids, but their feet are so heavy they cannot rise into the sky.'

'Tomorrow I shall speak to Moon,' said Sun with a yawn. 'She has a daughter; and though she is poorer than us, Moon's child dwells in the heavens and will make you a worthy bride.'

As day dawned, Sun rose early, just as his neighbour Moon was about to take her rest.

'I have found a worthy husband for your daughter,' he said; 'none other than my son Peivalke.'

Moon's bright face grew dim. 'My child is still too young,' she said. 'A puff of wind would bear her off. How can such a child wed your son?'

'It matters not,' said Sun. 'We will nourish her and make her strong. Come, give her to me.'

'No!' cried Moon, swiftly drawing a veil about her child. 'Your son would scorch her tender skin.'

'Remember, neighbour,' exclaimed Sun angrily, 'I am all-powerful: I give life to everything.'

'Your power,' said Moon, 'is but half the power that is. When dusk comes your powers recede into the night. Where is your power throughout the dark night?' At this Sun flew into a rage. 'Your daughter shall wed my son, whatever you say!'

Thunder rolled across the heavens, the wind howled, waves hissed and towered white with fury, herds of reindeer huddled close and the people trembled in their tents.

As Moon hurried away into the night, she muttered to herself, 'I must hide my child, keep her safe from Sun's fiery gaze.'

Looking down from the sky she spied a tent where a young Saami couple lived; they had no children of their own.

'To those earth people,' said Moon, 'I'll entrust my child; she will be safe with them.'

Next morning the man and woman were going to the forest to

strip birch bark for sandals, when they heard a tiny voice crying above them. 'Niekia, Niekia! Help me, help me.'

And there in the branches of a fir tree they saw a silver cradle rocking to and fro. As the man reached up to take it down, he saw a child lying there; she was like any other save she was as pale as moonlight.

They carried the cradle home and brought the child up as their own daughter, calling her Niekia – the first word they had heard her speak. As the days passed, Niekia grew into a tall, slender maid with plaits strung like silver threads. And every night, before she went to bed, she would leave the tent, raise her pale face and arms to Mother Moon and shine more brightly than before.

In the passage of time, however, Sun heard of the strange maid living among the Saami; and he sent his son to seek her out. No sooner did Peivalke gaze upon the lovely maid than he fell deeply in love with her.

'Earth maiden,' he said, 'try on these golden boots.'

Niekia blushed, but did as she was bid. At once, she cried out in pain,

'Oh, they burn my feet!'

Before his eyes she melted to a silvery mist – and the golden boots stood empty upon the ground. Wrapped in moonbeams, Niekia hid in the forest until nightfall. Then, as Mother Moon rose in the sky, she followed her mother's light through the trees and across the cold tundra. At last, as dawn was breaking, she came to the shores of a mighty ocean; and there on the strand was a lonely hut.

Niekia went in and found it empty; it was so untidy, she washed it clean with sea water. Her work done, she fell asleep in a corner of the hut.

As twilight cast dark shadows upon the shore, heavy footsteps woke her up and she saw a band of warriors enter, all wearing silver armour, each more handsome than the next. They were the Northern Lights led by their eldest brother Nainas.

'Our home is so clean,' said Nainas in amazement. 'A good housewife has visited us; I can feel her keen gaze.'

The brothers sat down to supper and, when they had finished, they began a mock sword battle, striking white sparks and scarlet flashes that danced and soared into the sky. Then, tired of sword play, they sang songs before flying off across the ocean; only Nainas remained.

'Now, dear housewife,' said Nainas, 'please show yourself. Should you be old, you may be mother to us. Should you be of middle years, you may be our sister; and should you be young, you may be my bride.'

'Here I am, judge for yourself,' said a voice behind him.

As Nainas turned, he saw a slender figure standing in the dim light of early dawn; and he recognized Moon's lovely daughter.

'Will you be my wife, Niekia?' he asked.

'Yes, Nainas,' she replied, so quietly he could barely catch her words.

At that moment the first pink flush of dawn spread through the sky as Sun's head appeared.

'Wait for me here, Niekia,' cried Nainas, and he was gone.

Every evening, Nainas and his brothers returned to their home on the shore, fought their sword battles and then, at sunrise, flew away again.

'Please stay with me for just one day,' Niekia begged Nainas.

'That I cannot,' he replied. 'For Sun would kill me with his shafts of fire.'

When the brothers had gone, Niekia had an idea: she would make a quilt of reindeer hide and embroider on it the stars and Milky Way, hanging the quilt below the ceiling of the hut.

So it was. When Nainas flew home with his brother warriors that evening, they played their games, ate supper, sang songs and lay down to rest. Nainas slept soundly; several times he opened his eyes but, on seeing the starlit sky above him, he thought it must still be night and went back to sleep.

Niekia was so happy. Just before dawn she crept out of the hut to prepare breakfast; but she forgot to close the door. And when Nainas opened his eyes, he saw the bright light of morning streaming through the door and Sun's golden sledge climbing up the sky. He dashed from the hut, calling his brothers after him.

But it was too late.

Sun sent down a shaft of fire that pinned him to the ground. Poor Niekia now realized what she had done. As swiftly as she could, she ran to Nainas, shielding him with her body. Slowly, he struggled to his feet and flew off to safety in the heavens.

Sun was furious. He seized Niekia by her plait, scorched her with his fiery gaze and summoned his son Peivalke.

'Now, will you marry my son?' he raged.

'You may burn me to a cinder,' Niekia said, 'but I will never wed Peivalke.'

'Then you shall marry no one!' said Sun.

With that he flung the girl high in the sky where Mother Moon caught her, pressed her to her bosom and tended her wounds.

She still holds her safely to this day. If you look closely at the moon, you will see the shadow of Niekia's fair face upon her mother's breast. She is watching the battle of the Northern Lights across the evening sky, and pining for her beloved Nainas.

The Little Master Thief

❦ N O R S E ❧

There was once a man who had six sons. When the eldest was eighteen and the youngest twelve, their father sent them out into the world to learn a trade. Off they went together until they arrived at the parting of the ways: the road went off in six directions. As each son prepared to go his own way, they agreed to meet there in two years before returning home.

Two years passed by, the six sons met and went home to their father.

'Well, my sons,' the father said, 'what have you learned?'

The oldest said he knew how to build ships that could sail all by themselves. The next said he could steer a ship over land as well as sea. The third son said he had learned to listen so well he could hear what was happening in the neighbouring land. The fourth had become a sharpshooter who never missed the mark. The fifth could climb any mountain.

The father was content.

'And you, my youngest son?' he asked.

'Father, I have learned to become a master thief,' the sixth son answered with a smile.

When the father heard that, he flew into a rage.

'Shame on you!' he cried. 'You bring disgrace upon me.'

Now it so happened that soon after a wicked wizard carried off the king's fair daughter; and the king promised half his realm and the princess's hand to the man who could save her.

When the six brothers heard, they decided to try their luck. The eldest built a ship that sailed by itself, the next steered it over land and sea. Keen Ears listened carefully and heard the wizard moving about inside a glass mountain. The climber swiftly reached the mountain top and saw the wizard asleep, his head on the princess's lap. Then he hurried back down and, taking the little master thief upon his back, climbed up the inside of the glass mountain.

When they reached the sleeping wizard, the master thief stole the princess so cleverly from under the wizard's nose that he did not notice a thing.

As soon as they were all aboard, the seven of them sailed away. Keen Ears was told to warn them should the wizard awake and come in pursuit. All at once, he shouted, 'The wizard has discovered the princess is gone. He is coming after us!'

The princess was beside herself.

'Oh dear,' she cried, 'we'll all be killed when the wizard catches us; the only way is to kill him first. He can only be killed by shooting an arrow at a tiny spot the size of a pinhead in the centre of his chest!'

Hardly had she finished speaking than the wizard came rushing through the air. In an instant the sharpshooter fitted an arrow to his bow, took careful aim and fired. The arrow sped to its mark and the wizard burst into a thousand fiery pieces – what we now call meteorites.

At last the six brothers came before the king with the princess; all had fallen in love with her, and each could truthfully say that without his help she would not have been saved.

What was the king to do? Even the princess declared she did not know which brother she loved best.

But the Great Spirit in the Sky solved the problem for them. During the night he turned the princess and six brothers into stars: they form the constellation that we call the Pleiades. And of the seven stars, the brightest is the lovely princess; the faintest is the little master thief.

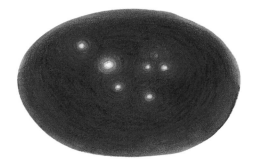

Perseus and Andromeda

The land of Ethiopia was once ruled by a king and queen called Cepheus and Cassiopeia; and they had an only daughter, Andromeda. One day the queen was foolish enough to boast that her daughter was more lovely than the Nereids – the lovely sea nymphs protected by the sea god Poseidon.

Beautiful as she was, the princess could not compare with the Nereids; and Poseidon would not forgive the queen for her idle boast.

As punishment he sent a huge sea serpent, Cetus, to devour anyone who ventured out to sea. So the fishermen could not sail their boats and starvation threatened the land.

When King Cepheus consulted his wise men, they told him, 'The only way to calm Poseidon's fury is to sacrifice what you love best.'

It did not take the king long to realize what that meant.

'I love my daughter most of all,' he sadly said.

There clearly was no choice. In great sorrow, the king and queen had to watch as their daughter was chained to a rock not far from shore.

At around that time, the young god Perseus, son of Zeus, father of the gods, was flying over Egypt eastwards towards Ethiopia. On his journey he suddenly saw the lovely maiden chained to a rock, her dark hair streaming in the breeze. Tears flowed down her lovely cheeks as the cruel sea crashed against the ledge on which she lay.

So moved was Perseus by her plight that he flew down to the shore. Andromeda's parents stood, gazing helplessly at the rock. No one surely could save their daughter from the serpent's jaws.

When Perseus heard the story, he vowed, 'I will rescue her and

slay the monster. In my pouch I have the
head of the hideous snake-woman Medusa; it
can turn anyone to stone merely by looking at them.
And when I'm done, I'll take your daughter as my wife.'

The king and queen readily agreed.

'But first you must kill the monster,' said the king.

Right at that moment, frightened shouts echoed along the
shore.

'It's coming! The serpent is coming!'

People were pointing to the churning, foaming waves on the
horizon. Perseus rose straight into the air, clutching his sharp
sword. As the onlookers stood in awe, he hovered over
Andromeda's rock, awaiting the great sea beast.

In a few moments, they could clearly see the beast; its huge
tail was thrashing the water into snowy foam, the swirling of its
coils made great eddies in the sea, and plumes of water hissed
from its nostrils. The waves that raced to shore smashed the little
fishing boats to pieces.

The evil monster did not notice Perseus approaching from behind, hanging over it like an eagle about to dive on its prey.

All at once, the young god plunged his sword into the flesh just behind the serpent's scaly head. Cetus reared up, stung by the blow, and lashed at Perseus with its tail. But the god rose high in the air, just in time to avoid its deadly sting.

Again and again he struck at the serpent until the dark blue sea had turned to crimson foam from the serpent's blood. At last, with a groaning and hissing, the monster rose from the water, then sank back, vanishing forever into the seething sea.

All the onlookers gave a great shout of joy. The king and queen were overcome with happiness: their daughter was saved. Alighting on the rock to unchain Andromeda, Perseus then bore her to the shore.

'I've kept my word and slain the serpent,' he cried. 'Now I claim my bride.'

Andromeda's parents arranged the wedding without delay. There was good cause for haste. For just as the guests were toasting the health of the happy pair, the doors of the palace burst open. And in rushed a great band of men armed with spears and swords.

It was the army of Prince Phineus.

'Andromeda is promised to me!' Phineus cried. 'I come to claim her.'

'Is this true?' asked Perseus, turning to the king.

'Sadly it is,' the king replied, red with shame. 'My daughter was promised to this man.'

Turning to Phineus, the king said sternly, 'But you forfeited that right when you left my daughter to her fate. She now belongs to Perseus.'

'Then he shall die!' cried Phineus.

It was an uneven battle. Since Phineus's army far outnumbered the king's men, the fight soon began to go against them. Suddenly, Perseus leapt upon a table and called out for all to hear,

'Let all who are my friends turn their gaze away!'

So saying, he pulled Medusa's head from his goatskin pouch and held it in the air. It truly was a terrible sight: a woman's face with black staring eyes and writhing snakes for hair.

'Your trickery does not deceive us!' shouted Phineus.

'Then look closely,' said Perseus, 'and you shall forever be a stone image of a coward.'

Perseus forced him to look full into Medusa's eyes.

Instantly, Phineus became a stone statue aiming a spear.

Perseus had won his bride and soon took her home to Greece.

If you look into the night sky, you may see Perseus, a constellation in the Milky Way. He is wearing a peaked cap; with one hand he is beckoning to Andromeda, with the other he is rescuing her from the rock. The chain that fastened Andromeda to the rock is dangling from her outstretched arm. Just below her is the mouth of the sea serpent Cetus sent to devour her.

Seventh Day of the Seventh Moon

◆ CHINA ◆

Long, long ago in a land beyond the stars there lived a fair princess, the only daughter of the Jade Emperor, Yu Huang. Each day she would weave delicate patterns on rugs and clothes and tablecloths. The Emperor was very proud of his clever daughter and often watched her in silent admiration.

'There is no greater happiness,' he thought, 'than to have a daughter who works so hard.'

One day, as he looked on, he was surprised to see the face of a young man appear upon her cloth. At first he was angry, but he realized that his daughter was a little girl no longer; she had become a lovely young woman and it was only natural that her thoughts should turn to men.

The princess, however, wept with shame; her fingers had betrayed her thoughts – for she had intended to weave a pattern of flowers for her father.

'Don't cry,' her father said. 'I'll find a husband for you who will make you happy.'

So the Jade Emperor summoned his wise men and commanded them to find the perfect husband for his daughter. After consulting for several days, a choice was made.

'We have found the ideal husband for the princess,' announced the wisest of the wise. 'He is a handsome prince from the next realm. Since he likes herding cattle, he is known as the Herdsman. What could be better: Weaver and Herdsman?'

An envoy was duly sent to the neighbouring realm and, as fortune would have it, the prince's father was delighted with the proposition. He too thought it the perfect match and his stargazers pronounced the omens right for the pair. A wedding date was set and the realms began preparing for the event. As was the custom, both sets of parents advised the children on their roles as man and wife.

'Be true to each other, work hard and always obey your parents. Then you will find perfect happiness.'

At last the happy day arrived and Weaver married Herdsman. There was not a more contented and devoted couple anywhere in the universe. They were so in love that they wished only to be together and gaze into each other's eyes. They played games all day long, sometimes lying in each other's arms and counting the stars.

Weaver's loom grew rusty for want of use. Herdsman's cattle grew skinny for lack of food. As the weeks passed into months, the Jade Emperor came to hear of their idleness and he sent for them at once.

'Your parents instructed you to work hard and be obedient,' he shouted. 'Yet all you do is play the whole day long, counting stars, running about the meadows and picking flowers. From now on you will live apart: you, daughter, will weave in the west of the realm, while you, son-in-law, will take your cattle to the east.'

The loving pair were overcome with grief. They wept for so many days and nights in their separate realms that the Emperor finally relented. He sent word that they could meet just once a year beside the Silvery Stream, on the seventh day of the seventh moon.

A year went by. The seventh day of the seventh moon arrived – the one night in the year when they could be together. With fast-beating hearts, each set out on the journey across the skies to the Silvery Stream. Yet when they arrived on opposite banks, they found that the Stream was so wide they could barely see each other on the distant shore. There was neither bridge nor boat.

In desperation the two lovers stared across the water. They cried and cried, and their tears fell to earth as rain, flooding the land below and threatening to wash away the homes of birds and beasts.

The animals called a council.

'We must do something before we all drown,' grumbled the black bear.

'Let's ask the wise old owl,' barked the fox. 'He'll know what to do.'

So all the birds and the beasts gathered beneath the bough on which the owl sat.

'The only way to stem the flood of tears is to help them across the Silvery Stream,' he concluded gravely.

A gloomy silence descended. Then, all at once, a little voice chirped up.

'I know,' said the magpie, 'why don't the crows and magpies make a bridge for them?'

It was worth a try. The sky turned black as all the crows and magpies flew up into the sky; up and up they soared until they reached the heavens. On and on they flew until they came to the Silvery Stream. Then, with their wings spread wide, they formed a bridge across the glistening waters of the Stream.

When the two lovers next gazed through tear-filled eyes, they stared in amazement. For where none had been before there was a bridge. In a trice, the Weaver Princess ran lightly across the wing-span bridge and threw herself into her husband's arms.

All night long they held each other in a fond embrace. Yet as dawn began to break, they had to part once more and she ran sadly across the bridge. Shedding a few last tears, they each made their lonely way to their east-west homes.

From that time on, the people living on the earth noticed a change at that time of year. There are always light drops of rain in the early morning as the two lovers weep on parting; and you will never see a crow or magpie on the seventh day of the seventh moon. If you do see them on the following day, mark well their loss of feathers: for they lost them as the Weaver Princess stepped lightly upon their heads while crossing the Silvery Stream – so that she could be with her husband for one night of the year.

And if you look up at the sky on the seventh day of the seventh moon, the seventh of July, you will see two bright stars, Weaver and Herdsman, in the early evening on either side of the Silvery Stream – what some call the Milky Way.

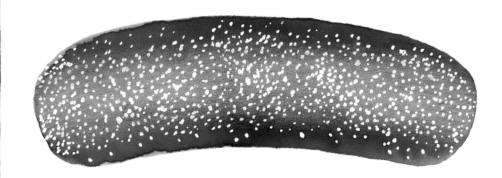

Sources

The Storytelling Star is a story told by the Seneca tribe in northern
America. It is based on 'The origin of stories' in Ella Elizabeth Clark,
Indian Legends of Canada (McClelland and Stewart, Toronto, 1960).

Birth of the Stars is an ancient Inca tale from South America. It is from a
Russian publication of Inca folktales collected by Oscar Alfaro, *Rozhdenie
zvyozd. Skazki* (*Birth of the Stars. Folktales*) (Moscow, 1984).

The Loving Moon Star comes from the Chippewa nation which has its
cultural roots in the central regions of Canada. The story is a mixture of
'The lover star' and 'The first white water lily' in Ella Clark. See also my
The Songs My Paddle Sings. Native American Legends (Pavilion, London,
1996).

The Girl Who Would Be the Sun is another story told before the Spaniards came to South America, when the Aztecs had their empire centred on Tenochtitlan (now Mexico City). This legend is taken from Carleton Beals, *Stories told by the Aztecs* (Abelard-Schuman, New York, 1970).

How Light Came into the World is a Maori creation myth from what is now New Zealand. See A W Reed, *Wonder Tales of Maoriland* (A H and A W Reed, Wellington, 1964)

Battle of the Northern Lights is one of the many beautiful folktales of the Saami people (Laplanders) who recognize no boundaries as they trek across Scandinavia and the White Sea coastline of Russia. I have translated the story from A. Yelagina, *Khozyaika travy. Saamskie skazki* (Moscow, 1973); it is contained in my Siberian folktale collection *The Sun Maiden and the Crescent Moon* (Canongate, Edinburgh, 1989).

The Little Master Thief is an old Norse story told by the Norsemen or Vikings and brought to western Europe from Scandinavia in the 9th century. See Barbara Leonie Picard, *Tales of the Norse Gods and Heroes* (Oxford University Press, London, 1953).

Perseus and Andromeda comes from the Ancient Greek, being one of the many adventures of Zeus's son, Perseus. Versions of the tale are contained in Robert Graves, *Greek Myths* (Cassell, London, 1955); and in A R Hope Moncrieff, *Classical Mythology* (George Harrap, London, 1907).

Seventh Day of the Seventh Moon is a story common to a number of ethnic groups in Asia, particularly the Chinese and the Koreans who both claim it as their own. See *Folk Tales from China*, fourth series (Seagull Publishing Company, Hong Kong, nd); and Suzanne Crowder Han, *Korean Folk and Fairy Tales* (Hollym, New Jersey, 1991). See also my *Korean Folk-tales* (Oxford University Press, 1994).